A LITTLE FLOWER SHOP

$\mathcal{I}$n a pretty blue house on Cobble Street, three girls named Rosie, Lily, and Tess lived with their Aunt Lucy. Rosie and Lily were sisters and Tess was their cousin, and while the girls' parents—who were dancers with the ballet—were touring the world for a year, the girls were all having a wonderful time staying with Aunt Lucy.

1

When Aunt Lucy went off to her flower shop each morning, the cousins walked together to fourth grade at a sturdy brick school on Olive Street. After school, they walked home and amused themselves while they waited for Aunt Lucy to close the shop and join them.

It was on a sunny afternoon in October as the cousins were playing with Rosie's paper

dolls that Lily had an idea. (Lily was very good
with ideas. She wanted to be a writer when
she grew up—a poet—so she listened for ideas
in her head all the time.)

"I think we need a project," she said.

"What sort of project?" asked Tess, putting a
yellow shawl across the shoulders of her doll.

"Well, here we are, all together, looking for things to do every afternoon," said Lily. "So I think we should make something. Something amazing."

Rosie, who was very domestic and loved being at home for any reason at all, said, "That's a great idea. But what?"

Lily leaned in toward the girls with a look of cheerful conspiracy in her eyes.

"Let's make Aunt Lucy a flower shop," she said.

"For goodness sakes, Lily, Aunt Lucy already has a flower shop," said Tess, rolling her eyes dramatically. Tess often rolled her eyes, for she hoped to be on Broadway some-day and thought it was good practice.

"No, I mean like a little dollhouse," said Lily. "Except it will be a little flower shop."

"That's a *wonderful* idea," said Rosie. "We can make little pots and tiny flowers."

"And a white picket fence along the front," said Lily.

"We can even make Aunt Lucy," said Tess. "And *Michael*!"

The cousins giggled in delight. Michael and Aunt Lucy were sweethearts, and it was all because the cousins had sold Michael some cookies in the summer and introduced him to Aunt Lucy. Michael was very sweet and kind to the girls, and they all hoped he'd marry Aunt Lucy someday.

"Let's make a list of things we'll need," said Lily. "I'll get my fountain pen."

Lily always used her fountain pen for important writing. She wrote all her poems with it, and letters to her parents, and thoughts in her journal.

She kept her pen and papers under a little wicker bed in the attic. The cousins all had "rooms" of their own in Aunt Lucy's attic. Lily's room, in the middle of the attic, was surrounded by lacy yellow curtains. Rosie's room, on the south end, was behind a lovely old patchwork quilt. And Tess's room, on the north end, was tucked behind a screen decorated with palm trees. Each girl had her own special things in her room, and each respected the others' privacy.

But a large part of the attic was set aside for The Playground, as Lily had named it, and here the cousins spread pillows and blankets, watercolors and brushes, comic books and paperbacks, dolls and stuffed toys, and here they made all their plans.

When Aunt Lucy came home
the girls were still so busy with
their lists and designs that
they almost didn't
want to stop
for tea.

But they
loved having tea
with Aunt Lucy every
afternoon, and not even for a
wonderful idea would they miss it.

The cousins ran downstairs to join her
in the parlor. Aunt Lucy was young and very
pretty. She had long red hair and freckled skin,

and she wore such colorful clothes: bright
pink jumpers, lime green jackets, blouses with
glittery moons and stars. But Aunt Lucy's
house was completely old-fashioned and her
parlor was, as Lily described it, "quaintly
quaint."

The girls sat in white wicker chairs and balanced their teacups and saucers on their laps while Aunt Lucy told them about her day. Elliott—Tess's black and white cat who lived in the attic, too—wandered into the room and rubbed against Aunt Lucy's legs as she talked.

"The sweetest old gentleman came by the shop today," said Aunt Lucy. "He wanted to send his wife something special to celebrate the day they first met, at an ice-cream parlor.

"So I went to French's Market and bought some cones and sprinkles, and I filled each cone with a white carnation. A little glue and choco- late sprinkles, some greenery and bows—it was an ice-cream bouquet!"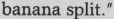

"Yum," said Tess. "Makes me want a banana split."

"Where do you buy all the little decorating things you use, Aunt Lucy?" asked Lily, giving Rosie and Tess a "pay attention" look.

"Oh, here and there. But the place I like best is The Olde Craft Shoppe over on Vine."

"Near Michael's apartment?" grinned Rosie.

Aunt Lucy blushed.

"Well, yes, but I liked it best *before* I met him," she said with an embarrassed smile.

"Are the decorating things expensive?" asked Lily, still gathering serious information.

"Oh no," said Aunt Lucy. "There are boxes and boxes of small loose things, old things and new things, and some cost as little as a penny apiece."

Lily and Tess looked at each other and nodded. They knew just where to head tomorrow after school.

"Do you think you'll marry Michael?" Rosie asked Aunt Lucy.

"Oh my goodness!" said Aunt Lucy, all flustered. "Heavens!"

"Is that a yes?" asked Tess.

The cousins giggled and giggled. Then Aunt Lucy smiled and kissed them all and cleared away the tea tray. She was still bright pink as she headed toward the kitchen.

SMALL THINGS

*I*f we're going to the craft shop, we have to stop and see Michael," said Rosie the next day. Of the three cousins, Rosie was the most particularly fond of Michael. She loved sweet, gentle people who smiled at her.

The girls were walking directly from school over to Vine, and each had a book bag across her shoulders.

"Ugh," said Tess. "Of all days, I had to pick

this one to borrow an atlas from the library. My bag is so heavy."

"Why do you need an atlas?" asked Lily.

"Well, when *I* go on tour someday," said Tess, "I want to know where I'm going. So I thought I'd start to get to know the world."

Tess loved to sing, and she felt sure she would be a performer one day. She collected old records of all kinds—opera, blues, jazz, show tunes—and she knew the words to every song she owned. Sometimes, when Lily and Rosie were bored, Tess would sing a number for them.

"I don't want to know the world," said Rosie. "I want to live on Cobble Street forever."

"Well, Mother and Dad definitely won't like that," said Lily. "They want us to travel the globe, like they're doing."

"I'd rather stay home and sew," said Rosie.

Lily and Tess giggled.

"Rosie, you are such a . . . a . . . a *Rosie!*" said Tess.

Rosie grinned. It wasn't such a bad thing to be.

The cousins saw Michael's apartment building, flanked by the two stone lions, just ahead.

"Please, let's just ring and see if he wants
company," said Rosie. "With Mrs. Haverstock
back in Chicago, he has no one to talk to."

Mrs. Haverstock, Michael's sister, had
stayed with him for a while in the summer

because Michael had fallen and broken his leg. But now Mrs. Haverstock had returned to her husband and three Scottie dogs in Chicago.

"All right, we can stop," said Lily. "Let's tell him about making the flower shop."

"And about Aunt Lucy saying 'Heavens!' and 'Oh my goodness!'" giggled Tess.

The girls stepped inside the door and rang the bell for Apartment 5.

"Yes?" said Michael's voice.

"Roses are red

Violets are blue

Cousins are here

To see only you," said Lily.

"Good poem, Lily," said Michael. "Hi, girls. Come on in."

Michael buzzed the girls into the hallway and was waiting for them when they reached the door of Apartment 5.

"Are you studying?" asked Rosie. "Are we intruding?"

"Yes, I'm studying and *please* intrude," said Michael, stepping aside. Michael was studying to be a botanist. Anyone could tell that he loved botany, for his living room was filled to overflowing with plants and trees. Michael's family was wealthy—in fact, his father owned the elegant apartment building—but Michael

wasn't interested in the family fortune. He wanted simply to be a botanist.

Michael was definitely the perfect match for the young woman who owned Lucy's Flowers. At least, the cousins thought so.

The girls told Michael about their flower shop idea and asked if he'd like to come along to the craft shop.

"Well, I shouldn't," said Michael. "I have a big exam in a couple of days."

"But," he said, smiling at the girls, "I could use an ice-cream cone. Can we make two stops?"

"I can't believe you said that," said Tess. "I've been craving a banana split since yesterday."

"Great," said Michael. "Let's go."

When the cousins and Michael reached the The Olde Craft Shoppe, things were not as they expected.

A tiny wrinkled woman was rushing about on the sidewalk, looking up into the trees and toward the roofs of the buildings.

"Oh no, oh no," she was saying. "Poor Petey, poor little Petey."

"Is anything wrong, ma'am?" asked Michael.

"My parrot escaped," said the woman. "I'm always so careful, but today, I don't know how it happened . . . Petey flew right out the window."

The woman pointed to the small apartment building next to the shop. A curtain fluttered through an open window.

Michael and the girls arched their necks to look as far up into the trees as they could.

"I don't see him," said Michael.

26

"Neither do I," said Tess.

"Nope," said Lily.

"Is he green and yellow with a fancy head?" asked Rosie.

"*Yes!*" said the tiny woman. "Where is he?"

Rosie pointed to an antiques shop across the street.

"He's on the rooster," she said.

Everyone looked. Sure enough, there was Petey on the rooster weather vane above the antiques shop. There was a slight breeze, and Petey was slowly spinning around and around. He seemed to be having quite a good time.

"Petey!" called the tiny woman. "Petey, you come home right now!"

Petey just ignored her and kept spinning.

Michael looked at the cousins.

"Why don't I walk over there and see if I can help coax Petey down? You girls can do your shopping and meet me when you're finished."

The cousins were very reluctant to leave all the excitement outside, but they knew that Aunt Lucy would be expecting them home in an hour. And there was still ice cream to squeeze in . . . .

"Okay," said Tess. "But come in and get us if something *remarkable* happens."

"I promise," said Michael. He followed the tiny woman across the street, heading for Petey.

The Olde Craft Shoppe was wonderful. There were big tables covered with dozens of little boxes of *everything*.

"It's like a fairyland flea market," said Lily, running her hands through a box of tiny silver stars.

"I love it," said Rosie.

"Me too," said Tess.

And they forgot all about Petey.

It took the cousins about twenty minutes to find everything they needed. If they could have stayed all afternoon, they surely would have.

But, with several little bags of small wonderful things, they finally stepped outside in search of Michael and Petey.

Michael and the tiny woman were still standing under the weather vane, looking up. And Petey was still spinning.

"Petey's having a fun day," said Rosie as the cousins joined Michael.

"Petey!" called the tiny woman. "Petey, you come home right now!"

"Did you get everything you need?" Michael asked the girls.

"Yes, and more," said Lily. "It was wonderful. Miniature teapots and tiny wheelbarrows and the sweetest little wicker chairs."

"I bought some glitter," said Tess. "I'm going to scatter it in my hair for my next performance."

"And I bought some beautiful silver thread, to repair my bear, Henry," said Rosie, digging into one of her bags. "See?"

She held out a silvery spool for Michael to see.

And just then . . . *flappa-flappa-flappa-PECK!* Petey flew down and with his beak plucked the spool of thread right out of Rosie's hand!

"Eeek!" squealed Rosie.

"Hey!" yelled Tess.

"Petey!" scolded the tiny woman.

They all watched as Petey
circled above their heads with his
wonderful prize. And then, slowly
and rather casually, he turned and
flew right back into his apartment.

"Yay!" clapped the cousins.

"Oh thank goodness," said the tiny woman.

"You'd better run right in and close that
window," said Michael.

"Oh yes, oh yes," the tiny woman said, hurrying away. "Little girl, I'll buy you another spool of thread."

"That's all right," called Michael. "No need! Happy to help!"

He turned to Rosie.

"Let's buy another spool, Rosie," he said. "I'll pay for it."

Rosie smiled.

"I'd rather you pay for a chocolate fudge cone with sprinkles."

Michael laughed.

"*Double* sprinkles," he said. "Maybe even triple."

Rosie took Michael's hand, and
everyone walked happily to the ice cream
parlor, talking, of course, of nothing but Petey.

SURPRISE!

Lily, Rosie, and Tess worked secretly on Aunt Lucy's flower shop for several days. First they cut pieces of cardboard and glued them into the shape of the building. Then they gave the cardboard two thick coats of white paint. Finally they began the fun part: decorating.

Because they hadn't any color photographs of Aunt Lucy's *real* flower shop, the cousins sometimes forgot exactly what it looked like.

When this happened—and it was daytime—
one of the girls would dash down to the corner
and take a good look at the shop. (Was the
bench on the right or left side of the door?)
Then she would run home with the information and the girls would begin again.

As they worked on the little shop, the cousins talked of all sorts of things. Whom they most admired, which books they liked best, where they wanted to take a vacation. And, as always, they talked of what they wanted to be.

"All of this making things on a budget is good for me," said Lily. "Because poets are

always poor. They live in tiny apartments above movie houses or cafés. And their friends all worry about them and bring them food. When I'm a poet, I'll have some practice making do."

"Well," said Tess, "I definitely do *not* want to be poor and this 'making do' is a good reminder for me. It reminds me that when I'm a Broadway star, I want to be *loaded*." She gave a mischievous grin.

The girls worked quietly a moment. Then Lily asked, "What about you, Rosie?"

Rosie looked up from the tiny chimney she was intently gluing on.

"Oh," she said, "this reminds *me* that I like to play with glue."

Lily and Tess giggled and giggled. Rosie said the most sensible things, but they always came out funny.

Finally by Saturday the flower shop was finished and the girls invited Michael over to share in their surprise. When Aunt Lucy arrived home from shopping, all four were sitting on the front porch.

"Michael!" exclaimed Aunt Lucy. "It's so nice to see you!" Aunt Lucy was looking very pretty. Her long red hair was in a ponytail, and she wore big silver hoop earrings.

The cousins could see that Michael really liked Aunt Lucy. He always turned so pink and clumsy when she showed up.

Michael reached out to help with Aunt Lucy's bags and nearly dropped them. The cousins looked at each other and smiled.

"The girls tell me they have a surprise for you," said Michael, holding the bags and the door open for Aunt Lucy. "I haven't seen it. I just hope its name isn't Petey."

Rosie giggled.

"At least I'd get my spool of thread back," she said.

Once the bags were put away and Aunt Lucy and Michael were settled on the front porch swing, the cousins had Aunt Lucy hide her eyes as they carried out the little flower shop. Then she looked.

"Oh my gracious!" she said. "It's my flower shop! Oh my goodness!"

The shop was glued to a flat board. Aunt Lucy picked it up and turned it around and around.

"Oh, you sweet girls," she said. "It's *beautiful!*"

And it was. It had the blue-painted window boxes and bold yellow door of Aunt Lucy's shop. It had the green park bench in front and the wishing well by the gate. It had windows

that said LUCY'S FLOWERS and a little sign that
said OPEN. And—best of all—it had Aunt Lucy!
There she was, a little wooden doll with long
red yarn for hair and a polka-dot dress.

Michael smiled at Aunt Lucy.

"It looks just like you," he said. "And I mean that in a good way."

"We have one more little surprise," said Tess.

She pulled something from her pocket.

A Michael doll!

"Yikes," said Michael.

The doll had Michael's messy hair and baggy sport coat—and in its hand was a tiny book that said *Botany*.

"Does my hair really look like that?" asked Michael.

"Yes," said Lily. "And I mean that in a good way."

Everybody laughed.

"Now if you get lonely, Aunt Lucy," said Rosie, "you can have Michael visit you." Rosie walked the Michael doll up to the shop door.

"Hmmm," said Aunt Lucy. "Too bad he doesn't have a box of chocolates in his *other* hand!"

"Oops. Guess we'll just have to make a trip back to The Olde Craft Shoppe," Tess said, grinning.

"Actually, I would love to go back there," said Lily. "There were some pretty lace doilies I could write poems on."

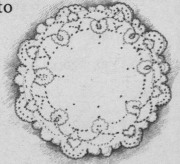

"And I could get more thread," said Rosie. "Henry Bear's arm is still loose."

"I'd like some big feathers," said Tess. "For my next performance."

"Why don't we all go?" said Michael. "And I'll spring for ice cream on the way home."

"Great!" said the girls.

So everyone walked over to Vine Street and The Olde Craft Shoppe. This time Petey wasn't riding on the rooster, so the street was very peaceful and the girls were able to browse in the shop for a long time. Michael was very patient. He occupied himself with a box of miniature trains while everyone explored.

Then, after stopping for ice cream as promised, they all walked back to Michael's apartment for tea. Michael loved exotic teas, so the cousins always had to try something new and strange, like Ginger Licorice Mint or Maple Tangerine. But the girls liked Michael so much that they didn't mind. And he always let them sit on his dragon bench with their teacups.

When the cousins and Aunt Lucy finally returned home, everyone was so tired. They all wanted a nap. Aunt Lucy hugged each girl tight and thanked them all again for being such sweet angels. Then the cousins went up to the attic and snuggled into their own beds.

Behind the long, lacy yellow curtains, Lily said, "Tomorrow I'll write everyone a little poem on a doily."

"And I," called Tess, "will make us some crazy hats with big feathers."

Things were quiet.

Then Rosie said, "Let me know if anyone needs an arm sewn back on."

Lily and Tess giggled and giggled.

"I meant your *toys*," called Rosie.

And everyone went to sleep with a smile.